11/99

SP

D0605167

X

92

COOL ALi

In memory of my father, Stanley Livingston Gordon

Margaret K. McElderry Books
An imprint of Simon & Schuster Children's Publishing Division
1230 Avenue of the Americas
New York, New York 10020

Copyright © 1996 by Nancy Poydar

Book design by Angela Carlino

The text of this book is set in Matt Medium Text 4
The illustrations were rendered in watercolor, oil pastel, pastel pencil, and colored pencil

Printed in Hong Kong by South China Printing Company (1988) Ltd.

First Edition

10 9 8 7 6 5 4 3 2 1

Library of Congress Cataloging-in-Publication Data
Poydar, Nancy.
Cool Ali / written and illustrated by Nancy Poydar.—1st ed.
p.   cm.
Summary: A young girl's chalk drawings bring her neighbors some relief on a hot summer day.
[1. Drawing—Fiction. 2. Summer—Fiction. 3. City and town life—Fiction.]
I. Title
PZ7.P8846Co   1996
E—dc20
95-35213
CIP
AC
ISBN 0-689-80755-4

COOL ALi

Written and illustrated by
Nancy Poydar

MARGARET K. MCELDERRY BOOKS

Ali loved to draw. She drew all the time.

One summer day, her mother said, "Ali, Ali, it's just too hot to be indoors!"

That's when Ali took her box of fat chalk outside.

It hadn't rained in weeks, so Ali drew grasses and flowers on the sidewalk. She was so busy she didn't notice other people coming out of the hot building. Some complained about the temperature. Some made newspaper fans.

The babies fussed.
No one could get
their mind off the
heat.

Then, Ali drew a little lake
around Mrs. Frye's chair.
"My!" sighed Mrs. Frye as
she kicked off her sandals
and wiggled her toes.
"My, my!"

"Cool," piped up Ira Baker,
squinting in the sunlight.

That was when Ali drew the
beach umbrella over Ira's head.
"Cool!" he said again.

Mr. Boyle put down his newspaper fan and looked around to see what was so cool on such a hot day.

There was no more room in the lake or under the beach umbrella.

Mr. Boyle looked into the hot haze and complained, "Not even a breeze, not even a breeze."

That was when Ali drew the North Wind. Mr. Boyle's teeth began to chatter. "Brrr," he said. "Brrr," mimicked the babies. "Brrr, brrr!"

Ali drew a polar bear with pale yellow fur. "Grrr," he seemed to say. "Grrr, grrr!"

"Wheee," squealed the babies as they took turns riding on his back. "Wheee!"

"What a day," said Ali's mother,
finally coming out of the hot building.
"What a day!" she said when she saw what Ali
had done! Then, she tested the water, admired the
beach umbrella, bowed before the North Wind, and
stayed out of the polar bear's way.

"Ali, soon you'll
have everything
covered!" she cried.
   That was when
Ali got the coolest
idea of all.

She began by drawing little
snow dots on the wall and
the sidewalk,

little snow dots around
the big feet and little
feet . . .

. . . little snow dots all over the lake and the beach umbrella. She drew polar bear paw prints and icicles, too.

She drew and she drew and she drew.

"My, my!" sighed Mrs. Frye.

"Cool!" said Ira Baker.

"Brrr!" chattered Mr. Boyle.

"Wheee!" squealed the babies.

"OOOO!" said the gathering crowd, thrilled
to be chilled to the bone!

No wonder no one noticed a little breeze rippling the haze and turning the leaves inside out. No wonder no one noticed the darkening sky or the first big drops of cold rain.

No one noticed until it pinged on the porches,
drummed on the mailbox at the curb, and hissed off
the hot sidewalk.

Then, it poured. Mrs. Frye did a jig with Mr. Boyle.

The babies opened their mouths to catch the rain, and Ira Baker splashed in the first puddles that formed.

Only Ali noticed the sidewalk pictures blotch, dribble, and stream brightly into the rushing gutter.

Raging blizzard, polar bear, North Wind, beach
umbrella, and little lake all washed away.
"Oh, no," Ali moaned. "Oh, no!"

But the crowd noticed Ali, whose drawing beat the heat. They clapped, they cheered, and they lifted her onto the tallest shoulders.

"Ali, Ali!" they chanted.

Ali loved to draw. She drew all the time.
Sometimes it was just too wet to draw outdoors.